ROBIN HOOD

✦AND THE✦

GOLDEN ARROW

Based on the
Traditional English Ballad

Retold by Robert D. San Souci

Illustrations by E. B. Lewis

ORCHARD BOOKS / NEW YORK
AN IMPRINT OF SCHOLASTIC INC.

 **Long ago in England**, when King Henry the Second ruled, there lived a great archer named Robin Hood. He spent his days and nights with his band of Merry Men in Sherwood Forest. Robin Hood, Friar Tuck, Allan a' Dale, Little John, and the others dressed in green to hide easily in the woods. They were known as heroes who helped all in need, always outsmarting the evil Sheriff of Nottingham.

The Sheriff vowed to capture Robin and his band. So he came up with a plan. He called for his men and said, "There is to be an archery contest with an arrow of pure gold as the prize. Robin Hood and his fellows will try to win the treasure; then we will arrest them." The others agreed that this was a clever way to catch the outlaws.

Word of the contest spread far and wide. When Robin heard about the prize, he told his fellows, "The Sheriff has sent a challenge we cannot ignore. No one can match us with bow and arrow."

Friar Tuck warned, "This is a trick of the Sheriff's to trap you."

But Robin's mind was made up, so he asked, "Who has a plan to let us enter the contest safely?"

Wise Little John said, "We must go disguised, and enter the town one by one from different directions."

On the day of the contest, Robin and his men traded their familiar green outfits for clothes in other colors. Robin dressed as a beggar in red rags, with an eye patch, and dyed his yellow hair and beard brown. Then the band set out for town by different ways.

The Sheriff viewed the event from his seat on a magnificent milk white horse. At his signal, the first archers took aim at the targets. All the while, the Sheriff and his spies watched eagerly for fellows dressed in green, but it was the only color not on the field that day.

Disappointed, the Sheriff studied all the archers, and then said, "That beggar is as tall as Robin Hood. But his rags are red, he is half blind, and his beard is the wrong color."

After several rounds, only two archers remained: Robin and the Sheriff's favorite, Gilbert.

Someone in the crowd shouted, "Only Robin Hood could shoot better than these fellows!"

Angry at hearing such praise, the Sheriff cried, "The outlaw is a coward who doesn't dare show his face. He knows these brave bowmen are better than he."

Robin whispered to Friar Tuck, "Soon the Sheriff will eat his words."

Gilbert, the Sheriff's man, fitted his final arrow to his bowstring, took careful aim, and loosed the shaft. It flew straight and lodged but a hairbreadth from dead center. The crowd cheered, and the Sheriff, smiling proudly, applauded Gilbert.

Then the beggar in red drew his bow, held the arrow a moment, sighted the target, and let fly. To everyone's amazement, his arrow struck dead center—so near Gilbert's shaft that it shaved off part of one feather. The stranger had won!

So the Sheriff had to present the golden arrow to the red-clad beggar. As he did, he asked, "What is your name, and where do you come from?"

"I am Jock of Greendale," the man answered.

"Well, Jock, I can always use a fine archer. Will you work for me?"

But the beggar merely replied, "I will remain my own master."

The Sheriff stormed off, with his men following. Meanwhile, Robin and his Merry Men took different routes back to Sherwood Forest, ever watchful for spies. When they met again in the greenwood, they roasted wild boar and praised Robin's success. But Robin said, "The victory will not be complete until we let the Sheriff know who won his prize."

So Allan a' Dale wrote a brief poem, which was carefully tied to an arrow. Then the merry group, still disguised, hurried back to Nottingham. Outside the great hall where the Sheriff sat feasting, Robin climbed to the top of the garden wall. Then he shot the arrow with the note through a tall, brightly lit window. The shaft buried itself in the table just as the Sheriff was preparing to carve a plump goose.

Furious, the Sheriff snatched the poem, which one of his servants had untied and held out to him. Growing red with rage, he read:

Your Lordship, now the tale is told,
From highest hall to deepest wood—
That today you gave your arrow of gold
To the greatest archer—Robin Hood.

Robin and his men listened to the Sheriff bellowing a few moments longer. Then, laughing, they returned to Sherwood, where many more adventures awaited them.

For Robert and Claudia,
whose friendship has always been
unfailingly on the mark
—R.D.S.S.

To my family for their love and support
—E.B.L.

Text copyright © 2010 by Robert D. San Souci
Illustrations copyright © 2010 by E. B. Lewis

Library of Congress Cataloging-in-Publication Data

San Souci, Robert D.
Robin Hood and the golden arrow / retold by Robert San Souci ; illustrations by E. B. Lewis.—1st ed.
p. cm.
Summary: Retells, in easy text, the Sheriff of Nottingham's plot to hold an archery contest in order to capture the
outlaw Robin Hood, but Robin and his band of merry men arrive in disguise with a plan of their own.
ISBN 978-0-439-62538-8 (reinforced lib. bdg.)
1. Robin Hood (Legendary character)—Legends. [1. Robin Hood (Legendary character)—Legends.
2. Folklore—England.] I. Lewis, Earl B., ill. II. Title.
PZ8.1.S227Rob 2010   [398.2]—dc22   2009015624
10 9 8 7 6 5 4 3 2 1   10 11 12 13 14
Reinforced Binding for Library Use
First edition, October 2010
Printed in Singapore   46
The artwork was created using watercolor on Arches 300lb cold press paper.
The book was set in Perpetua.
Book design by Lillie Howard

AUTHOR'S NOTE

The preceding tale is based mainly on the traditional British ballad (a narrative poem usually intended to be sung) "Robin Hood and the Golden Arrow." It was first presented in the Child Ballads, a collection of over 300 traditional songs from England and Scotland, compiled by Francis James Child in the late nineteenth century.

A large part of that work focuses on songs about Robin Hood. These sung story-poems often took their inspiration from older sources. "The Golden Arrow" had roots in the tale "A Gest of Robyn Hode," written around 1450 and also collected in the Child Ballads. In it, Robin Hood and his disguised Merry Men compete in an archery contest, are recognized and pursued by the Sheriff of Nottingham, and barely escape.

The author also consulted *The Merry Adventures of Robin Hood of Great Renown in Nottinghamshire*. This 1883 novel by American author and illustrator Howard Pyle brought together many of the old tales, including "The Golden Arrow," into a single narrative geared to younger readers.